D1442010

APR -- 1997

THE BROKEN TUSK

Stories of the Hindu God Ganesha

Retold by
Uma Krishnaswami

with illustrations by
Maniam Selven

LINNET BOOKS 1996

Library of Congress Cataloging-in-Publication Data

Krishnaswami, Uma, 1956–
The broken tusk: stories of the Hindu god Ganesha /
retold by Uma Krishnaswami, with illustrations by
Maniam Selven.
p.   cm.
Summary: A collection of stories about the pantheon
of Hindu gods, centering on the sometimes greedy, sometimes impulsive, but always generous, elephant-headed Ganesha.
ISBN 0-208-02242-5 (alk. paper)
1. Ganesha (Hindu deity) — Juvenile literature.
[1. Ganesha (Hindu deity)   2. Mythology, Hindu.]
I. Selven, Maniam, ill.   II. Title.
BL1225.G34K85   1996
294.5'2113—dc20   96-22410

Designed by Abigail Johnston
Printed in the United States of America

To my parents

Contents

Preface

I began this book of stories about the elephant-headed Hindu god Ganesha by retelling as many stories as I could remember from my childhood years in India. My parents, grandparents, and other adults around me had spoken vividly and often of the people, gods, and demons in these stories, so that as a child I was sometimes unsure if they lived only in legend or down the road from us. I wasn't certain how I felt about all of them, but Ganesha I'd have been glad to meet, anytime! The process of recalling and retelling resulted in stories like "Kubera's Pride," "Ganesha's Head," and the first Ganesha tale I remember hearing at about age four, the one I have titled "The Broken Tusk."

Once I'd written down all the stories I knew, I began searching for materials to fill in the gaps in my knowledge. I read many books by scholars on Ganesha and Hinduism and talked at length with people familiar with the mythology surrounding Ganesha. I hoped they would lead me to some stories I had never heard of. From this search came stories such as "The Old Young Woman and Her Songs," "The Dance," and "Why Ganesha Never Married." Along the way, I was fascinated to find out that Ganesha strayed into some Buddhist myths from about the sixth century onward. I could not resist including one of them, the Mongolian legend, "The Birth of Phagpa."

When stories are handed down orally through the generations, they sometimes evolve into many different versions. For example, I know of at least five versions of the story of Ganesha's creation and how he got an elephant's head, and at least two versions of his encounter with Kubera. In each instance, I have selected the story that I thought might stand best on its own, without needing long explanations of the mythological web in which it is embedded.

Occasionally legends might seem to contradict one another or to present a confused picture of the entire mythology. For instance, in the story of "Ganesha's Head," Ganesha is created as a young child by Parvati, yet in "In the Beginning," he seems to exist in an adult form before anything else appears in the whole universe. Again, this can be best understood by remembering that these legends were not all written down at one time but evolved over many generations of people and across a geographical area of more than a million square miles.

In retelling the stories, I have tried hard to be faithful to traditional versions. There is a difference, however, between stories told face-to-face—in a language that is native to both storyteller and listener and with the storyteller close enough to touch—and those told in translation through the written word. For instance, in retelling these tales I have always called the elephant-headed god *Ganesha*. The traditional Hindu storyteller is just as likely to refer to him by any one of his other names—as I mention in "Ganesha's Head," he has one hundred and eight of them. I have included a list of some of them, with their meanings, at the back of this book. There is also more dialogue in my stories than there might be in any oral rendering. Finally, the sights, sounds, smells, and textures of the settings of these stories are those of the India and the Hindu tradition that I know. They are the filters through which I heard these tales, so I have used them in the retelling.

Ganesha

In legends of the Hindu people of India, Ganesha is a god with an elephant head and a human-like body. He is the son of Parvati, the goddess who takes many forms: mother, protector, ferocious destroyer of evil. His father is Shiva, who once saved the world by swallowing the poisons emerging from the ocean of milk when the gods and demons churned it. Ganesha is wise and fat, often impulsive, making an occasional mistake but always filling the world around him with laughter. He loves sweets and rides a tiny mouse.

Ganesha is sometimes shown with two arms and hands, sometimes with four; even, in one depiction, with ten. He holds many tools in his hands, and is usually pictured carrying some combination of these things:

- a goad, a type of hand-held spur used by elephant drivers. It is a symbol of the good judgment that urges people into good actions;

- a noose to snare obstacles and sweep them out of the paths of people;
- a *modaka* or sweet dumpling. The *modaka* is a symbol of joy;
- many kinds of weapons such as axes or swords or bows;
- the broken tusk, standing for sacrifice, from which the title of this book is drawn; the tusk also stands for literacy. The story, "The Broken Tusk" explains this odd meaning;
- a variety of fruit, including mangoes and pomegranates, representing prosperity and a plentiful harvest.

Tucked into the curl of Ganesha's trunk is a pot of water from the river Ganges or Ganga, which is sacred to Hindus and symbolizes purity.

Ganesha is associated with the sound *Om*, the sound of creation. In the ancient language of Sanskrit, the letter for *Om* [ॐ] looks rather like the head and trunk of an elephant. In the southern Indian language of Tamil, the symbol for this sound, although very different from the Sanskrit, also looks like an elephant's head with its trunk falling in a graceful curl [௲].

There is another emblem that has long been a symbol of Ganesha, and that was traditionally held in deep respect by Hindu people. Unhappily for Hindus, it is a symbol that was adopted by Hitler's German Third Reich in the 1930s and has come to stand for unspeakable evil and corruption to people of the Western world. This is the *swastika*, whose name in Sanskrit means, literally, "it is well," and whose arms, sweeping across the four directions, stand for continuity and the eternal cycle of life. In Hinduism, the *swastika* does not imply malice or exclusion. It can be seen on ancient granite statues of Ganesha in temples that are thousands of years old.

Ganesha is the "gate-keeper" at all temples of his father Shiva. Before you enter a Shiva temple, you must first pay your respects to Ganesha. Some say that if you rub the belly of a Ganesha statue, you will have good luck. People ask for his blessing before they begin a new job or set out on a journey. In many Hindu homes in India and in countries around the world, pictures or images of Ganesha decorate the entrances and are common household art objects. Ganesha watches over writers and merchants. When shops and offices go out of business, they announce the sad news to their customers by turning the office Ganesha statue upside down.

Once a year, Hindu people pay special respect to Ganesha. That day is called *Ganesha Chaturthi*, and it falls on the fourth night after the new moon in August or September (*chatur* in Sanskrit means "four"). The date varies from year to year because the calendars Hindus follow for religious holidays calculate the months differently from the Gregorian calendar, which is used in Western society. On this day, Ganesha images made of wood or clay—or in recent years, of painted papier-mâché—are taken in procession through many towns and cities. At the end of the day, the images are immersed in the nearest large body of water, to symbolize the return of all things to the elements. On the beaches of the west coast city of Bombay, hundreds of Ganesha images are cast into the waters of the Arabian Sea. The *modaka* or "sweet dumpling" that Ganesha loves is a special food for this holiday.

Ganesha appeared in Hindu art much earlier than in mythology. The oldest Ganesha image found by archaeologists is an imprint on a silver coin minted by an Indo-Greek ruler named Hermaeus in the first century B.C. On its reverse side the coin has the image of the Greek god Zeus. It was not until the fourth or fifth centuries A.D., though, that Ganesha images began appearing throughout the area we know today as the Indian subcontinent.

Through the centuries, how Ganesha has been shown in Hindu art has varied from one region of India to another. In the south Ganesha was always shown with his trusty companion, the mouse, Mushika. In parts of northern India and Nepal, he was sometimes also shown riding a lion, although there do not seem to be any surviving myths telling us more about his lion mount. In some ancient temple carvings Ganesha is even depicted in a female form called Ganeshini. Again, we have no myths to tell us more about these sculptures.

Like the sculptures and engravings, myths about Ganesha vary. In the northern part of the country, stories tell of his marriage to two wives, while in the south he is held to be a bachelor, as in the story, "Why Ganesha Never Married." His role as a scribe in "The Broken Tusk" is thought to have northern origins.

The Ganesha myth appears to have spread beyond India to Nepal and Thailand and even to places as far away as Cambodia, Borneo, China, and Japan, where Ganesha tales found their way into Buddhist mythology. In these stories Ganesha was commonly called by another of his Sanskrit names, *Vinayaka*, which means "supreme leader" or "one who has no other leader." In later Buddhist mythology, however, Ganesha was transformed into a villain trying to stop the spread of Buddhism. In Japan the Ganesha image was sometimes altered into that of twin elephant-headed gods called the *Kangi-ten*. The fragments of a statue found in China show Ganesha riding a tortoise. In both China and Japan, the broken tusk was occasionally shown as a radish with a leafy top, held in one of Ganesha's hands.

Only one story in this collection, "The Birth of Phagpa," is not a Hindu legend. It is from the Buddhist tradition called the *Mahayana* or "the Great Way," and comes not from India but from Mongolia. With this one exception, the stories in this book are tales of Ganesha that have been told by generations of Hindu people for hundreds of years. Many of them are told to Hindu children to this day.

Hindu Mythology

Hindu mythology is a vast and seamless fabric of legend. Its stories come from the many traditions of the peoples and cultures that came into contact with each other in the ancient world of the Indian subcontinent. Like deposits left by ocean waves upon the seashore, each invading or trading or intermingling culture left its mark upon the mythology we now know as Hindu.

In world mythology, we find traditions such as the Norse or Greek whose legends have survived to enrich us, even though they have no links to present-day religious practices. In contrast, Hindu myths form the folklore of the nearly one billion people around the world who call themselves Hindus. While the Hindu religion, of course, includes far more than its folklore, these stories are a rich and central part of the Hindu way of looking at life.

There are three worlds in Hindu mythology. The first is peopled by gods or *devas*; the second by demons or *asuras*; and the third by human beings. Conflicts between the *devas* and *asuras* are frequent and form the plots of many Hindu myths. But *asuras* sometimes pray and meditate and become very powerful, and *devas* are sometimes foolish and make mischief on earth.

Indra, the king of the *devas*, is a colorful but not very powerful character in Hindu mythology. He was probably much more important in early Hinduism than he grew to be in its later centuries. Although Indra now holds a secondary place among the Hindu gods, there are many stories told about him. He rides a six-tusked white elephant named Airavata. In one version of the legend, the elephant who donated his head to Ganesha is Airavata's son.

Much more important among the gods are Brahma, Vishnu, and Shiva, who are sometimes referred to as the Trinity of Hindu gods.

According to Hindu legend, Brahma is the creator of the universe, or of many universes, each of which is formed, exists, and dies within each cycle of creation. Brahma lives in a lotus flower that emerges from Vishnu's navel at the beginning of each age. He awakens and then creates the universe. Brahma was chief among the priests who performed the ceremonies for the marriage of Ganesha's parents, Shiva and Parvati. His wife is Saraswati, goddess of knowledge and learning. In art, Brahma is shown with four heads, each facing in a different direction.

Vishnu, the god who preserves and sustains the universe, sleeps on the coils of a giant serpent with a thousand heads called Adisesha. From Vishnu's navel grows the lotus on which Brahma sits. Once Brahma creates the universe, Vishnu comes to the world of people in one of his ten forms or incarnations to preserve order and ensure justice. This is one of the cycles of creation. At its end, Shiva dances and the universe is destroyed. Brahma falls asleep, and the lotus closes and goes back into Vishnu's navel. Vishnu sleeps on Adisesha's coils. Then the process begins all over again. The universes exist rather like endless reflections in a looking-glass, each image representing different times and circumstances. Hindu mythology says that we are in the tenth of these cycles now.

Shiva is the god of destruction and disintegration, both seen as necessary forces in Hinduism. It is Shiva who dances the dance that ends each cycle of creation. In Shiva the universe sleeps at the end of each cycle, before the creation of the next one. Although he lives in the icy northern mountains, Shiva is restless and roams over all creation. He is often depicted as a hermit, body smeared with ashes, wearing the skin of a tiger and with a glowing crescent moon in his matted locks. Sometimes he wanders through funeral grounds where the bodies of the dead are cremated, and the ghouls and creatures of darkness are among his followers.

All the gods in Hindu mythology have magical powers. They can bestow wonderful blessings or terrible curses on each other, as well as on *asuras* and people. All of them, as well, can change their physical forms and take different shapes, in order to solve a problem or teach a lesson.

People in the legends are, of course, just people. They are sometimes wise and sometimes stupid. They spend their days loving, hating, caring, destroying—doing all the things they have done throughout the ages on this earth. Among them we find kings and servants, and we find *rishis*. A *rishi* is a holy man who has gained great powers and wisdom through fasting, prayer, meditation, and *yoga*. A *rishi* in legend is most likely to live in a forest, on a mountainside, on a riverbank, or in a hermitage known as an *ashrama*.

Meditation, or quiet contemplation of the divine, which is practiced by many Hindus even today, is a recurring theme in these stories. Seated quietly, legs crossed into the position called "the lotus" and eyes closed, the individual shuts out the material world in order to focus on the deepest truth. In the Hindu tradition, meditation is often a part of the practice of *yoga*, and can lead to the attainment of great knowledge and power through conquest of the individual's physical needs.

Hindu tales sometimes refer to many cycles of life. Just as Hinduism views the universe as existing in endless cycles, in which worlds are born, exist, die, and are born again, it also teaches that souls are born, live and die, and are born again, literally, into other bodies. This is a frequent theme in Hindu stories. The next life is earned by the *karma*, or deeds of the present one, until the soul has achieved its greatest learning. Characters who have attained great wisdom, or made great sacrifices—like the elephant who gave his head to Ganesha—are released from the cycle of life and death, and their spirits can then join with the pure energy that forms the spirit of the universe.

Like all peoples through the ages, ancient Hindus asked the question, "How did it all begin?" There are several versions of the Hindu myth of creation. The one I have included stars Ganesha, and comes from the 2,000-year-old tradition of a people called the Ganapathyas, who believe Ganesha to be the most sacred of the gods. Other versions of the Hindu creation legend do not feature Ganesha at all, and most are quite different from this one.

There was a time when Hindu religion, philosophy, art, and science were not separate from each other, but were intertwined to form the basis for a way of life. Tales of Ganesha tell of the arts, of healing, and of the Hindu people's view of the cosmos. The plants and herbs referred to in some of the stories in this book hint at the linkage between the arts and sciences and the daily lives of people. For example, the species of basil, *tulasi*, that is used even today in wedding ceremonies, is also offered to deities in temples. In traditional medicine, it is used as a remedy for colds and fevers. *Durva* grass, used in worshipping Ganesha, is similarly believed to have both spiritual and medicinal properties.

Myths in Hinduism are often told to teach a way of life, to take difficult ideas and present them through symbols and through characters—the gods, demons, and people who represent these ideas. There are hundreds of gods in Hindu mythology: gods of nature; gods of the arts and the deeds of people; gods who symbolize various aspects of human nature, heroes, and ancestors; and many, many others. Yet Hinduism says that the many gods are all symbolic of one universal spirit, which is also called *Brahman*. The *Vedas*, which are part of the Hindu scriptures, put it this way: "Truth is one. The sages call it by many names." Fortunately for the world, the characters who manifest truth in Hindu legend are rich and colorful—and many. Their stories, like the Ganesha tales in this book, sparkle with their many reflections.

मूषिक वाहन मोदक हस्त
चामर कर्ण विलंबित सूत्र ।
वामन रूप महेश्वर पुत्र
विघ्न विनायक पाद नमस्ते ॥

Mushika vahana modaka hastha
Chamara karna vilambita sutra
Vamana roopa Maheshwara putra
Vighna Vinayaka pada namaste

Riding a mouse, *modaka* sweet in hand
Large ears like fans, wearing a long sacred thread
Short in height, son of Maheshwara (Shiva)
Lord of obstacles, I bow at your feet.

Ganesha's Head

On the mountain called *Kailasa*, among swirling mists and deep, dark shadows, lived the great god Shiva. He loved the snowy peaks all around his home, and the giant ice-caves that yawned on their frosty slopes. Sometimes, after a long and tiring hunt, he would spend hours sitting cross-legged in the snow, lost in his deepest thoughts. Sometimes the hours stretched into days.

One such day, when Shiva was away, his wife, Parvati, grew tired of being alone in their mountain hut. "I wish I had someone here to keep me company," she said out loud.

"Company -ny -ny," came the echo from the mountains.

"I know," said Parvati. "I'll make a doll out of clay."

Parvati got busy. She scraped clay from the earth. She wet it. She molded it. She shaped it with care. She made the figure of a child, a plump little boy with a laughing face. His eyes seemed to look right into her own.

"You could almost be alive!" exclaimed Parvati. "Wait— perhaps I shall make you live, little one."

Then Parvati inhaled and gently, gently, blew the breath of life into the clay doll. The doll was at once transformed into a child, with raven hair and dimpled cheeks and shining eyes. He stretched sleepily and smiled at her.

"I have no child," said Parvati to the laughing boy. "Be my child, small one, and I will love you."

The little boy was playful and strong. When he danced in the forest, the animals danced with him. He called Parvati *Amma*, which means "mother." When she saw his glowing smile, her own face beamed with happiness.

Days went by. Shiva had not come back. One morning, Parvati said to her child, "I'm going to take a bath. Stand guard at the door, child. I don't want to be disturbed. Don't let anyone in."

The little boy picked up a spear and stood at the door, ready to stop all who might dare enter. He pursed his lips. He knitted his brows. He made his face as fierce as it could look.

Suddenly, Shiva rushed in, draped in tiger-skin, the cold, thin crescent moon tucked in his tumbled hair. An icy cold draft of air rushed in with him, and the fire warming the little hut sizzled and died. Shiva tried to brush past the boy, but the child still gripped his spear tightly, even though the stern god's presence filled him with fear and the sudden cold made his breath hang like mist in front of his face.

"You can't go in," said the boy. "I won't let you. My mother said I mustn't let anyone in."

Shiva laughed. "Your mother? Who are you? How dare you talk to me like that? Let me in, little monkey. I want to talk to my wife."

The boy pointed his spear at Shiva. "No," he said. "Not until my *Amma* is done with her bath."

Now Shiva had a terrible temper, and this stubborn child made him angry. His rage erupted. It was so fierce that the day grew dark and giant gray clouds tore across the face of the sun. Shiva lost all reason. He lifted his hunter's axe high over his head, and with one swift blow he chopped off the little boy's head.

"What's all this noise about?" cried Parvati, rushing out. Then she gave a great scream of horror. "You have killed my son!"

"Your son?" said Shiva. "You have no son."

But Parvati wept. "I had a son, and you have killed him." Through her tears she told her husband the story of the child's creation.

3

Then Shiva's hot temper cooled. "Oh, my wife," he lamented, "what a dark and terrible thing I have done."

"Go now," said Parvati to Shiva, "and find the head. If you fetch it quickly and fix it back on my son's body, he may yet live."

Shiva began to search for the head. But his blow had been so mighty that the boy's head had been thrown up into the air. Flying like the swiftest arrow, it had landed deep in the forest. Hunt as he might, Shiva could not find it. Tired and sad, he sat on a fallen tree trunk with his head in his hands.

An elephant passing by saw Shiva and asked him, "O king of the dance, why are you so sad?"

"I have done a dreadful thing," said Shiva. "Anger filled my heart, and I killed a small and innocent child. I cut off his head, and now it is lost."

The elephant said, "Lord of the world, my years are many, and I am ready for my next life. Take my head, and use it to make the child live again."

The elephant bent his old knees and touched his head to the ground at Shiva's feet, saying, "Cut it off quickly. I am not afraid of pain. I should be honored to have you send me to my new life."

Shiva said to the elephant, "Wise one, I thank you. May you be blessed. You need not be born to a new life, as all who live must. I set your spirit free, so you may join the *devas*, the gods." Golden light flashed and fragrant flowers bloomed as the soul of the elephant flew to the home of the *devas*.

With the elephant's head in his arms, Shiva raced back home. He touched the head to the child's dead body. Parvati laid her healing hands upon the child and, just as he had done when she first breathed life into him, the boy awoke. He stretched sleepily and smiled at her. Parvati hugged her child and wept with joy.

"Small one," said Shiva, "my heart has wept for you, and now I am glad. Because you were so brave a guard, I will make you the leader of the *ganas*, my followers, and your name shall be *Ganesha*. Your new head will make you as wise as you are strong and brave. From now on, people who receive your blessing before they start new tasks will have good luck. You shall remove obstacles from the paths of the people, and they will call you by many names."

That is how Ganesha got his elephant head. He has many names, one hundred and eight in all. One of them is *Gajamukha*, "Elephant-face."

Many temples in India, in honor of the old elephant's sacrifice, keep elephants as respected guests. Temple elephants are cared for lovingly and are fed sweet rice and sugarcane. On holy days they lead colorful processions through the towns and villages.

You Are the World

In time Shiva and Parvati had another child, and his name was *Muruga*. He had six heads because when he was an infant, he was cared for and nursed by the six mothers who live in the sky, in the group of stars we know today as the Pleiades. Muruga's face was bright like a star. He carried a lance of fire.

Muruga was brave and swift, but he was jealous of Ganesha. "He laughs so much, and everyone loves him," he grumbled.

"Child, you must live at peace with your brother," cautioned Parvati.

"He's too fat. He eats too much," complained Muruga.

"Nonsense," said Shiva. "He is your brother. You mustn't say hurtful things about him."

In the forests that cloaked Mount Kailasa lived many animals. The brothers were friends with all of them—tiger and leopard, hawk and snake and bear. Muruga's favorite was the peacock, proud and shining, with tail-feathers like the robes of a king. Muruga rode the peacock everywhere, and the peacock loved him dearly.

Ganesha's mount was a tiny mouse with a pink, trembling snout, beady eyes, little clawed feet that pattered on the ground, and a long rope of a tail.

"Foolish you look, brother, riding that tiny creature," scoffed Muruga. But the mouse loved Ganesha and managed to carry him wherever he wished.

One day, Ganesha and Muruga, arguing as usual, came home from the forest.

"You look like a mountain," said Muruga.

"And you are too vain," said Ganesha. "You and your peacock both."

"I'd rather die than be fat like you!"

"I'd rather be fat than a show-off!"

"My children, do not squabble," said their mother Parvati, offering them a dish of fruit. In the dish were blood-red pomegranates and dainty grapes of soft green and purple-black. And there was one, but only one, very special fruit. It was a mango, juicy, golden, plump, warm from the tree and scented like summer.

"The mango," said Ganesha and Muruga together, their hands reaching out at the same time for the one fruit.

"You did that on purpose," Muruga stamped his foot at his brother. "You don't even like mangoes that much. You're always stuffing yourself with pomegranates."

"Children, my children," soothed Parvati. "Must you always fight over everything? Why can't you just share this fruit?"

Ganesha and Muruga looked at each other, then at Parvati, then again at each other. Ganesha shrugged his shoulders. Muruga shook his head. "Share?" they both said. "No!"

"All right, I have an idea," rumbled Shiva. "If you must compete, let's have a real competition. The first one to go around the world gets the mango. Go on, we'll see who's faster."

Muruga yelled, "Oh, I know I am! Come, my peacock with eyes on your tail, take me around the world." He jumped up onto his elegant bird. Within moments he was lost in a flurry of dust and wind.

Ganesha stood still. He seemed to be lost in thought.

"Ganesha?" Parvati asked him. "Are you not going to join in this race?"

Ganesha smiled slowly. Then he placed his palms together in the gesture of greeting and respect, *namaste*, and walked, very slowly and steadily, around his parents. Then he held out his hand for the mango.

Shiva frowned. "What's this? Around the world, I thought I said."

"You are the world," Ganesha replied, respectfully. "You are mother and father to the universe. You are its life and breath. But most of all, you are the world to me." He knelt before them and bowing down, touched his head to their feet.

"Oh, you are clever." Muruga had returned to hear Ganesha's words. He was hot and tired. The fine feathers of his peacock were limp with exhaustion.

"Brother," said Muruga, when he had caught his breath, "I might be faster than you, but you're much, much cleverer than I am. Go ahead, the mango's yours."

Ganesha laughed in delight as the juice of the golden mango dribbled onto his ample belly. At his feet, the little mouse, Mushika, scurried about to catch the drops that fell to the ground.

The Cat

When Ganesha was a small child, he often amused himself by playing on the forested slopes of Mount Kailasa. Sometimes he would invent games, pretending to be a great king and leading imaginary warriors into battle. Once, having nothing to do, he said to his mother Parvati, "I have nothing to do."

Parvati looked surprised. "Nothing to do, with the mountains for your playground?" she remarked. "When my spirit is unsettled, or when my soul needs new vision, I sometimes go where the wild creatures go, to see the world through their eyes."

"I'll go out now," decided Ganesha, "but I will go hunting."

Ganesha looked around outside the hut. He

picked up a stout stick and a large flat rock with sharp edges. He tied the two together with lengths of vine. Brandishing his make-believe axe, he ran off, leaping down the mountain trails, shouting with glee, "I am the greatest hunter of all! Wild animals, run for your lives!"

Ganesha stopped and looked about him. "But what shall I hunt?" he said. "I need an animal to hunt."

Suddenly a cat darted out from behind a rock and ran off down the trail.

"Aha!" cried Ganesha. "I'm going to pretend you're a tiger, and I'm going to hunt you!" And he raced off after the cat.

The cat ran down the mountain, mewing with fright. But Ganesha was too caught up with his game to notice her fear. He had convinced himself she was a ferocious tiger, and he was determined to hunt her down.

When he caught up with her, he grabbed her by the tail and pinned her to the ground, shouting, "Now I've got you, you evil tiger!"

The poor cat was too afraid to do anything but lie very still. She could not even meow. She shivered and quaked, and all of a sudden Ganesha noticed that his fearsome prey appeared to have surrendered completely.

Sulkily, he let go of the cat's tail, and she ran off as fast as she could.

"That was no fun at all," muttered Ganesha, as he picked himself up and went back home. When he got there, he was surprised to find that his mother Parvati was covered with scratches and bruises, as if rocks and boulders had cut her skin and thorns had pierced her cheeks.

"*Amma*, what happened to you?" asked Ganesha, forgetting the disappointments of his own day.

"You did this to me, child," said Parvati to Ganesha. "Don't you remember?"

"I did?" Ganesha was horrified. "No, I didn't. I would never hurt you like that."

Parvati said, "Think back. Did you hurt a living creature, only a little while ago?"

Ganesha was about to deny this terrible accusation completely, but then he remembered the cat. He looked at the ground in shame. He hung his head lower and lower until his big ears drooped down to his chest and his trunk slumped on the earth.

"I was that cat," said Parvati. "Remember this for all your life. When you hurt any living creature, you hurt me."

Ganesha hugged his mother sadly. "Forgive me, my mother," he said. "I did not mean to hurt you."

"Ah, but did you mean to hurt the cat?" asked Parvati.

"No," said Ganesha. "Yes—I mean no, no, I didn't. It was only a game."

"For you, perhaps," said Parvati. "But as you can tell, it was no game for me. Take care that in your play you do not injure others or cause them grief and fear."

"Yes, *Amma*," promised Ganesha. After that he took special care to be gentle to the wild creatures of the forests and streams, as you must, too, for any one of them could be Parvati in disguise.

The Rhythm of the Moon

Ganesha was very fond of sweets. There was one that he especially adored, a dumpling called a *modaka*, which has a steamed wrapping made of rice flour and a filling that absolutely bursts with coconut and dried fruit. *Modakas* are sweetened with jaggery, which is rich and flavorful and made by drying the juice of the sugarcane. Whenever Ganesha saw a dish of *modakas*, he had to stop and eat one. Of course, once he had eaten one, he had to eat another. Then another, and another, until the dish, in no time at all, was empty.

One day, the people of the earth were preparing for a special feast. In a village house, someone had set out an enormous platter of *modakas* to cool.

"Aha!" cried Ganesha, following the aroma, his trunk twitching in delight. "My favorite food." He hurried past the low mud wall that stood around the thatched house, and slipped in through the small wooden gate. He set down the goad and the noose held in two of his hands, unclasped the other two, and began to help himself.

Soon even his tremendous belly was filled. Ganesha looked at the platter. "There are still some left," he remarked in surprise. He picked up the last few *modakas* and stuffed them into his mouth.

"That was good," he said, climbing on to Mushika's back. "Let us go." The mouse started up obediently.

At that very moment a snake slithered across the threshold. Mushika, startled, tripped, and his master went flying off his back.

Alas, Ganesha's great stomach was like a sack that is too full and can hold no more. When his body hit the ground, his stomach burst, spilling *modakas* in every direction.

"Oh master, forgive me," said the mouse. "You are hurt."

"Shhh," said Ganesha, reaching out for the spilled *modakas* and hurriedly trying to put them back into his stomach. "No one saw this happen."

Looking around for something to hold his belly together, he saw the snake, still in the doorway.

"The very thing," said Ganesha, and he picked up the snake

and tied it around his waist like a belt, to hold in the *modakas* and keep his belly closed.

Just then a loud chuckle broke the quiet. Chandra, the moon, had appeared in the sky in his silver robes, with the twenty-seven stars who were his wives. He peered in through a window and laughed out loud at Ganesha's plight. "You call yourself a mighty god! Just look at you, you greedy creature."

Ganesha's temper flared. He took the broken tusk that he often carried in one hand and flung it at the moon. "Go away!" he yelled.

All of a sudden it was dark. The silver disc of the moon, struck by the piece of broken tusk from Ganesha's angry hand, was gone. The sky was still and black. The stars trembled in fear and sudden loneliness. All creation seemed to stop in dismay at Ganesha's anger. Then the heavens burst with tears of rain. Even the *devas* pleaded, "Change your mind, O lord of planets. Undo what you have done."

"What have I done?" said Ganesha, suddenly coming to his senses. "I have destroyed the balance of day and night. How can I possibly restore rhythm to the universe?"

Ganesha was silent for a while, and then he said, "O Chandra, listen well, for this shall be the rhythm to which you will wander the skies. You shall grow larger every day, for fifteen days, until you are once more the glowing circle you were in the heavens. Then, to remind you not to mock others, you shall grow smaller for fifteen days, until, before you disappear, you shall look just like my broken tusk. This is how you must journey through the months, proud moon, over and over, for all time."

Then Ganesha gathered up his goad and his noose and his dignity. He picked up his piece of broken tusk from the ground where it had landed and mounted Mushika for the journey back to his mountain home. He was never quite as greedy again, and he still wears the snake around his middle. As for you on earth, remember this well. On the day of *Ganesha Chaturthi*, which comes around on the fourth night after the new moon every August or September, make sure you do not look at the moon. He will only just be coming out of hiding and deserves to be ignored on that day, for he feels ashamed of himself for laughing at Ganesha.

Kubera's Pride

Kubera was the god of wealth. His palace was filled with gold and precious gems and priceless works of art, rare and beautiful. The fountains of his gardens gushed perfume. At night, a thousand oil lamps threw dancing lights upon the statues in his marbled halls. He held great feasts in his palace, and his guests were welcomed into rooms panelled in gold and silver, the ceilings inlaid with rare jewels from the far corners of the earth.

All this wealth and luxury made Kubera very vain. "No one in the three worlds is as rich as I am," he boasted. "Nobody can entertain a noble guest with as much grace and taste as I can. The silken pillows in my palace are woven with the colors of the rainbow. My cooks serve feasts like no other. Nobody, nobody is as great as I."

Ganesha heard of Kubera's growing vanity. He chuckled to himself. "I'll teach that Kubera a lesson," said he. His belly shook with mirth.

"What's so funny?" asked Shiva.

But Ganesha only laughed louder. "I'm off for a while," he said to Shiva. "I shall tell you all about it when I return."

Ganesha took himself to Kubera's golden palace.

"Welcome, son of Parvati and Shiva," said Kubera. "Stay awhile, enjoy the beauty of my scented gardens. May I ask my musicians to delight your lotus ears with melody? What will you hear? A flute, perhaps, or strings?"

"That's all very well," said Ganesha. "Some good food was actually what I had in mind, Kubera. I have a hunger raging in my belly that even your fancy cooks might have trouble satisfying."

Kubera arched an eyebrow at Ganesha. "Indeed?" he said. "I think, Lord Ganesha, you speak without knowledge of the talents of my cooks. Wait here while I summon the master of my kitchens."

Kubera gave orders for a great feast to be prepared. "Spare no effort," he told the cooks. "Use the finest ingredients and the most delicate and fragrant spices: saffron from the valleys that hide among the Himalaya Mountains and cardamom from the tropical south." He cast a hasty glance at Ganesha's beaming face and ponderous belly. "Make plenty of everything," he added.

An army of cooks set to work in the kitchens of Kubera's palace. They scrubbed and washed. They chopped. They steamed. They boiled and rolled and fried. They stirred great pots with mighty iron ladles and scalded the milk from a hundred cows to make *pal payasam*, rice pudding rich with saffron and nuts.

Finally, the feast was ready. Ganesha's trunk twitched at the delicious aromas floating through the palace. Kubera's servants sprinkled the marble floors with rose-water. Tiptoeing around the enormous dining hall, they carefully arranged the broad green leaves of the banana plant from which the honored guest was to eat. Kubera clapped his hands, and huge gold dishes, piled high with mouth-watering food, were carried in on the shoulders of the servants.

Ganesha began to eat. He ate fast, then faster, then faster still. In a matter of minutes, the entire first course was gone.

"Good, good," rumbled Ganesha. "More, please."

"Bring on the second course," signalled Kubera.

Minutes later, the second course was gone. Then the third. The fourth, fifth, and sixth vanished in quick succession. "Kubera," beamed Ganesha. "This food is really delicious. Could I have some more?"

The servants wheeled in a great urn full of *pal payasam*. Ganesha waved everyone aside, dipped his trunk into the urn,

and drained it to the very last drop. "I could eat such a feast all night long," he exclaimed. "Could I trouble you for a little more?"

"Lord Kubera," whispered the head cook, "all we have left is a little rice. He has eaten as much as a hundred people could."

"Bring the rice, bring everything you have," hissed Kubera. "I can't let Ganesha tell the world that Kubera could not feed him properly."

Ganesha ate the rice, to the last grain. He ate uncooked rice from the pantry, and great sacks of lentils and grains as well. He ate the banana leaves on which his dinner had been served. He flopped his way into the kitchen and ate the firewood stacked by the door. He ate the serving ladles and the pots and pans. He ambled out into the garden and ate a few trees. "These banana trees are good," he said. "I think I'll try an orange tree for a change of flavor."

Ganesha drank the perfumed waters of the fountains, draining them quite dry. He was just starting to tear a door off its hinges for a snack, when Kubera caught up with him. "Ganesha," pleaded Kubera. "God of good fortune, stop, I beg you. Why are you doing this to me?"

Barely glancing Kubera's way, Ganesha continued his rampage, tearing through the palace and eating everything he could lay hands on. In desperation, Kubera prayed to Ganesha's father, Shiva. Instantly Shiva appeared, and surveyed the damage.

"Tell me the truth, Kubera." Shiva's voice was stern. "Did

you offer Ganesha a meal because you honor him? Or because you wished to show off your talented cooks and your beautiful palace?"

Kubera hung his head. In shame he went to Ganesha and bowed to him, saying, "You who wear the moon on your forehead, forgive me my pride. I offered you a meal out of vanity and not love, and so what I had to offer was nothing at all."

Shiva gave Ganesha a small handful of roasted rice. "This should satisfy your hunger for the moment," he said, smiling. "Spare the rest of Kubera's gardens, my son. You are giving him as big a headache as the bellyache he tried to give you."

Ganesha gave a mighty sigh. "I thought he'd never understand!" he cried. "Finally, I can stop eating." He popped the rice in his mouth and gave a gigantic burp. He nodded to Kubera and his open-mouthed attendants and summoned his mouse, Mushika. Waving his trunk in farewell, he set off on the long ride home.

The Broken Tusk

In ancient times there lived a sage, a wise and gifted poet whose name was Vyasa. One day a great and beautiful story came into his mind. "I must recite it soon," he said, as his fingers counted prayer beads made from the seeds of the holy *rudraksha* tree. "I feel it in my heart. I know that the verses will flow from my lips like nectar from a flower."

There was only one problem. "I have no scribe to write this story down," said Vyasa. "The words and rhythms tremble on my tongue. If I stop to write them, the rest of the story might die inside me, and that would be a terrible thing. I must find someone who can write it down as fast as I recite, so

26

that people who live long years from now can know this story."

Vyasa prayed to Brahma, the great god who created all things. Vyasa spent long hours in prayer. He prayed in silence and in song. He prayed in sunshine and in rain, in daylight and in darkness. He neither ate nor slept, and small ants built hills between his toes, and creeping vines began to climb up his body. In time Brahma appeared to him in a blaze of white light.

Vyasa opened his eyes, and they were bright and hot with the power of his meditation.

"Lord Brahma," said Vyasa. "I hold in my heart a story of great truth and wisdom, but I have no one to write it for me and for all the people through all time."

The unsung story seemed to hover in the air, like shimmering heat waves that dance above the rocks at summer's height. Brahma himself trembled as he felt its strength. "Ask Ganesha, the elephant-faced one," said Brahma. "He can make all obstacles disappear. He will surely help you." And Brahma vanished in his blaze of light.

Again, Vyasa prayed, this time to Ganesha. In a while, Ganesha appeared before him.

Vyasa implored, "O dancing god with the elephant head, who can hold the world in your great belly, do me the honor of being my scribe. Write down the story with which my mind overflows, so others may read it and learn from it."

"What is this story?" rumbled Ganesha.

Vyasa said, "It is the story of life and death, good and evil, war and peace."

Ganesha laughed, and his enormous belly shook. In lakes and ponds and temple tanks the pink and white lotus flowers burst into bloom and flooded the air with their magical scent. "Me?" he asked. "There are many stories in this world. No doubt yours is filled with marvels, but why ask me?"

"Lord of planets," said Vyasa, "problems and obstacles melt away when you come near. Help me."

Ganesha frowned, and the lotus blossoms closed and drooped and the clouds lowered. He laughed again, and the skies cleared. The flowers shook off water droplets and opened once more. "All right, Sage Vyasa," said Ganesha. "I'll be your scribe, but on one condition. In telling your story you must not rest or stop for any reason. If you do, I'll stop writing and go away, and the story will stay half-written."

Vyasa thought. At length he said, "You of the long trunk and lotus feet, I bow to you. But I, too, have a condition. I won't stop while I tell my story, but you must understand all that I sing, as I sing it. You must grasp every word before you write it."

"Oh, very well," said Ganesha. He laid down all the things he usually held in his four arms—goad and noose, sweet dumpling and axe. He set down the pot of sacred water from the river Ganga that nestled in the curl of his trunk. He crossed his mighty legs, adjusted the jewelled crescent moon on his forehead, and announced, "I am ready, most holy one."

Vyasa sat up straight. He cleared his throat, and began. "*Om!*" he chanted, singing the sound that is the sound of creation, the sound that the universe made when first it began. The note was deep and strong. It echoed up mountains and down valleys, until all the world knew that Vyasa had begun his story.

"*Om!*" chanted Vyasa, "listen. Long ago, when the ocean was milk, this story has its beginning . . ."

At the sound of Vyasa's story, the creatures of the earth grew silent and still. It was a story of cousins who loved and hated and fought each other, of power, of friends and enemies, joy and sadness. It was a story about life and everything it holds, both good and evil. For hundreds of days and hundreds of nights the story rang out. "Who hears this tale shall find with ease the path to eternal life," sang Vyasa. "Who tells it shall bestow a gift more precious than jewels."

All the time, as Vyasa chanted the verses, Ganesha wrote, fast and furious. Vyasa was careful not to pause, but as time went on he grew a little tired. So once in a while, just to give himself time to think about the next part of the story, he would throw in some difficult words or long, roundabout sentences. Ganesha, grumbling to himself, would have to stop a moment and try to understand what Vyasa had just said before writing it down. Sometimes, to make sure that Ganesha understood, Vyasa had to use many words of explanation.

Suddenly the rhythm of writing and listening, so much like

the ebb and flow of the tides, was rudely interrupted by a small, sharp cracking sound.

"My pen!" muttered Ganesha.

Worn with so much use, Ganesha's pen had broken. He looked around for something else with which to carry on his writing. Only soil and grasses were all around. Ganesha took a quick look at Vyasa. The poet was taking a deep breath, getting ready to begin the next verse.

Now, Ganesha had long, elegant tusks, polished and pearly-smooth, with fine sharp tips. Reaching for his right tusk, he quickly flexed his muscles and snapped it off. Without missing a stroke, he used the broken tusk to continue writing the verse that Vyasa had already begun to recite.

It took Vyasa three years and one hundred thousand verses to complete the tale. The *devas* and *asuras* and people who lived in the three worlds all gathered to listen. The sun and moon seemed to stand still to hear it.

At length the great poem came to an end, with the last faint echoes of the very last words. Now the *devas* showered rose petals on Vyasa. Ganesha yawned carelessly, stretched, and rubbed his great belly in satisfaction. People cheered. Music echoed through the skies. Even the *asuras*, enemies of the gods, were silent in amazement.

From that time to this, Hindu children are told tales from the *Mahabharata*, the story Vyasa dictated to Ganesha. They hear it at bedtime and at play. It tells of right and wrong, duty

and respect and loyalty. Statues of Ganesha, sculpted through many centuries, show him with a broken right tusk. He holds the broken piece in one hand, so that all people who see him might remember how Vyasa and Ganesha struck a bargain, and kept their promises to each other. As a result, one of Ganesha's names is *Ekadanta*, "One-tusk." Writers say he is their special friend and helps them when they have difficulty transforming their thoughts into words. And often in the jungle, old bull elephants who have lost a tusk remember him fondly.

Small and Swift

Once there was a demon, an *asura*, whose greed for power grew greater with each passing day. Like Ganesha, he too had the face of an elephant, but his was a curse, brought upon him by a sage he had once angered. He was called Gajamukhasura, which means "demon with the face of an elephant."

"Out of the way!" people would cry when Gajamukhasura came near, and they would run and hide until the very last trace of his shadow had passed by. The rage in his heart made his tongue bitter. His forehead was forever folded into a dark and brooding frown. Some said that when he walked the forest paths, the jasmine flowers would fall off their stalks in fright and the fish in ponds and lakes would dive head-first into the mud at the bottom and forget to breathe.

One day Gajamukhasura overheard some people talking about him. "Strange," said one man. "He looks so much like Ganesha, you would think he would want to be more like him."

"Ah, but Ganesha is full of joy. This one is gloomy like the dust-clouds of summer that bring no rain but only heat and misery," replied another. "How could he dream of competing with Ganesha, who fills our hearts with music and our souls with joy?"

"Who dares speak ill of me?" Gajamukhasura rushed out at the two men, sending them diving for cover into a clump of thorny bushes. He raised up his trunk and trumpeted, shrill and loud, "Ganesha, I, your enemy, am coming. I will trample you into the dust and then I will be the only one with an elephant head."

Howling out his anger for all the world to hear, Gajamukhasura thundered up the mountainside to Kailasa, where Shiva sat in meditation, legs folded into the lotus position, eyes closed.

"Come out, Ganesha!" shouted Gajamukhasura.

Ganesha poked his head around a clump of trees and inquired, "For what reason, good sir? What is your hurry? There are berries and fruits to eat and sunshine to enjoy."

Gajamukhasura's anger grew hot within him. His jealousy of Ganesha sent harsh words tumbling out of his mouth. "Ganesha, you are a coward with water in your veins," said he.

"You live in Shiva's shadow and pretend to be brave. Come out and prove yourself in battle."

"Battle?" said Ganesha mildly, considering a ripe banana for a moment before offering it to a passing monkey. "Oh, surely there's no need for that."

Gajamukhasura stamped his feet, sending a small avalanche hurtling down the mountain slopes. "Perhaps it's your famous father who's stopping you," he jeered. "Or is it your mother, behind whose robes you wish to hide?"

"Ganesha!" Shiva's voice cut through the mountain air like the edge of a sword. "Must I deal with this insolent fool or will you take care of him?"

Ganesha tore his eyes away from a bunch of berries hanging from a vine. "I suppose you'd better fight with me, if you must fight with someone," he said to Gajamukhasura. "There's no telling what will become of you if my father gets really angry." And Ganesha stretched out one of his four arms, the one that held his trusty broken tusk, and stepped lazily out into the path of the *asura*.

One moment Gajamukhasura was flexing his muscles and clenching his fists. The next he lay spread-eagled on his back on the ground, pinned by Ganesha's broken tusk, all the breath knocked out of him.

"How did you do that?" wondered Gajamukhasura, when he had recovered his voice. "I didn't even see you move."

Ganesha shrugged, and a laugh thundered up from his belly.

He bent down and picked up his broken tusk and helped the *asura* up. "Now what shall I do with you?" he said. "You are taking up far too much space on this beautiful mountain."

Gajamukhasura bent low and touched Ganesha's feet with worshipful hands. "Let me be your servant and follower," he said. "Forgive me my foolishness; I see I have much to learn from you."

"Oh?" Ganesha thought for a moment. "What is it exactly you wish to learn?"

"Your—your speed!" gasped the *asura*. "If I could move that fast but once in my life I would die happy."

Ganesha's eyes twinkled. "And you wish to serve me, you say?"

Gajamukhasura nodded eagerly.

"Would a different form suit you, do you think?" asked Ganesha. "It might be confusing to have two of us around with elephant heads. And there are other shapes that lend themselves better to speed."

Gajamukhasura bowed his head. "Any shape you choose would suit me, my lord Ganesha," he replied.

Ganesha narrowed his eyes in thought. Then he snapped his fingers. "I have it!" he cried. "A mouse! That's what you'll be, a mouse. Yes, you shall be small and clever and quick, and sharp-sighted. You shall move with the speed of the monsoon clouds, and together we shall travel the world. O Mushika with eyes as bright as stars, may you carry me to the far corners of the universe and share my joys and sorrows."

And all at once the giant demon Gajamukhasura was transformed into Mushika, the tiny gray mouse with jet-bright eyes and a long tail. He has served Ganesha faithfully ever since.

The Dance

Once, when Ganesha was just a youth, he was walking along a forest path, listening to the calls of the birds in the treetops and stretching his trunk to breathe in the warm, damp scents of summer. His feet dug into the soft green mosses of the forest floor. He pulled a piece of fruit off a tree branch and stuffed it carelessly into his mouth, swishing its juices over his tongue joyfully.

In his delight at this beautiful day, Ganesha forgot to look at the path ahead of him. Rounding a corner, he bumped into Brahma, who was walking, deep in thought, on his way to the river. The bump quite knocked the breath out of Brahma. Jolted rudely out of his pleasant reverie, Brahma glared at Ganesha.

"Son of Parvati," said Brahma, and the anger in his voice spilled out into the woodland summer, so that the ants hauling grains of rice to their anthills stopped in their tracks and trembled with fear. "Son of Parvati, I —"

But the curse he was about to pronounce upon this impudent youngster with an elephant head died before it was born—for Ganesha, seeing that Brahma was angry, had begun to dance. At first his big belly shook and his feet thudded noisily on the forest floor. The flowering creepers swung away in alarm, and hordes of chattering black-faced monkey mothers retreated to the very tops of the trees, gathering their small babies to their underbellies as they scurried up.

But as Ganesha concentrated, his fat body took on an elegance all its own, and his dance was as beautiful as the rhythm of the tides and the music of the stars. Brahma's frown, trying hard to stay on his face, melted away, and he broke into a smile.

"Truly you are a son of Shiva, Ganesha," said Brahma. "Like the strokes of a pen that end each verse of a poem, Shiva's dance ends each cycle of creation. But your dance—your dance has in it the laughter of creation itself, the joy of the universe."

Ganesha stamped and whirled, and the crescent moon glowed on his forehead. The birds sang in time, and the monkeys hammered out the beat on the tall tree trunks, "Tham—thakita—tham! Thai—thakita—thai!!"

Ganesha did a final whirl, ending with his feet planted squarely on the ground. He faced Brahma, laughing, and held his right hand, palm facing out, in the gesture of blessing called the *abhaya mudra*.

Brahma bowed down to Ganesha in respect. "You who are young, yet have such exquisite dancing in your soul, I bow to you. I was about to curse you for interrupting my thoughts, but now I bless you instead, O Ganesha. You will be known by people as the master of the dance. All who perform this art in town and in city, in temple and in court, must first invoke your blessing. May it be so, as long as the earth shall live."

Today, in the classical Indian dance style called *Bharatanatyam*, Ganesha's gesture of blessing, the *abhaya mudra*, means "be not afraid." Even today, every Bharatanatyam performance begins with a special brief dance that recalls Ganesha's grace and seeks his blessing.

In His Belly

One day, Brahma the Creator yawned. Out of his mouth fell a demon, who was red and smelled strongly. "Am I your child?" the demon asked Brahma, chucking him under the chin of one of his four heads, the one that faced north. "I must be, since I fell from your mouth into this world."

Brahma was sleepy and so did not realize what a terrible child this was. "You are, I suppose, my child," said Brahma. "Since you are such a splendid red, fiery-red, the red of the flame-tree blossom, I shall call you Sindura, after the red ocher rock."

"Will you grant me any wish I might have?" asked Sindura, puffing hot breath against Brahma's shoulder.

41

"Yes, yes," said Brahma sleepily, trying to brush aside this unruly new child of his.

Sindura roared with joy, making Brahma jump. Small flames licked out of Sindura's nostrils. Smoke curled out of his discus-shaped ears. Brahma looked at Sindura and was at once fully awake.

"I wish to be all-powerful," howled Sindura. "None shall defeat me. Everything I touch shall be consumed by fire. I shall burn up all my enemies, even you, if you cross my path, my so-wise and so-godly father. Although, of course, I shall burn you up with great regret and sorrow." He brought his face close to Brahma's and laughed out loud, so that Brahma pulled back in dismay.

Animals and birds all around had fled at the sound of Sindura's hideous laughter. The silence of doom to come was everywhere. The *devas* in their homes trembled with fear. Indra, their king, went to talk to Brahma.

"The *devas* are afraid," said Indra to Brahma. "You have given a deadly gift to this dangerous monster, and you must stop him."

"I too am worried," admitted Brahma. "I should have refused to grant his wish, or sent him to some faraway place where he could do no harm. But I was foolish and now nothing I can do will stop him. Perhaps Ganesha can help us."

So the *devas*, led by Brahma, went to Ganesha, who was relaxing on the slopes of Mount Kailasa after a light meal of honey and rice-cakes. "Help us, lord of laughter," said the *devas*. "Sindura is wrecking the worlds. Listen, you can hear the sounds of his terrible destruction."

Drifting up the peaceful mountain slopes were thunderous crashing sounds and the crackle of forests blazing. The acrid smell of smoking wood began to tickle Ganesha's senses. He lifted his trunk high and gave a hefty sneeze, "Aaahhh—aaahhh—aaahbushku!"

"Sindura, who's he?" said Ganesha, when he had recovered from his sneeze. "Burning up the world? Nonsense, we can't have him doing that. Just give me a moment." He reached for his noose and goad and his pot of water from the holy river Ganga.

"I'm ready," said he. "Lead me to this child who thinks he can destroy the world. I'll put a stop to him."

But Sindura was not so easily stopped. His fiery breath singed Ganesha's noose, and Ganesha was barely able to retrieve his precious goad before it began to melt in the white heat of Sindura's flaming laughter. Ganesha flung the Ganga water at Sindura. It made the demon pause for a brief moment, but then he gathered his strength and carried on, burning people and trees and houses with equal fury.

"Stop!" cried Ganesha. But Sindura only laughed louder.

Now the *devas* were in a panic. "Ganesha, remover of all obstacles, even you are powerless against this creature," they cried. "Truly, the universe must bow to his evil wishes. Doomed! We are all doomed!"

Ganesha, hearing their hopeless cries, gathered all the strength in his massive legs, his iron arms, his coiling, flexing trunk. He came close to Sindura. He opened his mouth until the demon could see the darkness of a yawning cave in it, and far inside, the twinkling of stars and the reeling of planets in their paths about the universe. As Sindura paused, for the briefest moment, Ganesha opened wider still and swallowed Sindura up, swallowed his fire-breath, his smoky, howling laughter, his shiny red face, just swallowed him.

The *devas* sucked in their breaths in amazement. Then they began to shout in dismay. Ganesha, far from digesting the demon, had fallen to the ground and was writhing in agony, as Sindura began to burn inside him.

"Quick!" cried Indra. "Bring Ganga here so she can cool this fire. If Sindura burns Ganesha up, the entire universe will burn. The planets in their courses will explode, and the stars will wink out, and all life will end."

The river Ganga gushed and frothed uphill to get to where Ganesha lay. Although her sparkling waters slowed Sindura's fire, it continued to burn.

"Ice, ice from the caves of Mount Kailasa," gasped Ganesha.

Shiva and Parvati brought massive chunks of ice, hewn from their mountain home where the snows live forever. "That helps, but I'm still on fire," muttered Ganesha. "Oh, my stomach!"

"Bring the moon to cool my son," ordered Parvati. Chandra the moon came, and cast his chilly rays upon Ganesha's fevered

body. But still Sindura burned inside Ganesha, and the moon quaked with fright.

"I cannot do much more," said Chandra. "If Sindura continues to destroy the universe, my time will soon be up, and I will burn with the other heavenly bodies."

A *rishi* who had spent years in the forests, and who knew the healing power of herbs and grasses, spoke up. "Lords, I am only a human, but I offer you this grass. Lay it on Ganesha's head, and it will quiet the fires within him."

Indra scoffed at the *rishi*, and said, "Go back to your forest and smear your body with ashes, O sage, and get ready for the end of the worlds. This fire is too strong for even Ganesha to smother."

"Wait," said Shiva. "What grass is this, holy one?"

The *rishi* bowed to Shiva, and joining his hands in respect, said to him, "Lord Shiva, you who rattle the drum of life and death, this grass is called *durva*. To many it is a weed, to be cast away and burned. But it has strength and grows true and sturdy, and it has power to heal." The *rishi* opened up his knotted waist-cloth, and offered Shiva a handful of three-bladed and five-bladed *durva* grasses.

Shiva placed the grasses on Ganesha's hot head. Slowly, slowly, Ganesha's pain receded. Slowly, slowly, his stomach ceased to burn. Slowly, very slowly, the fires went out, and Sindura became just another atom in the universe contained within Ganesha's belly.

Ganesha heaved a sigh of relief and mopped his sweating face. "Brahma, O Brahma," said Ganesha. "Do be careful the next time you grant a wish to anyone."

Brahma bowed his head and disappeared as quickly as he could.

"This grass is very special," said Ganesha to the *rishi*. "Is it hard to find?"

"It grows everywhere," said the *rishi*. "It is as common as sand."

"But more precious than gold," said Ganesha. "In all my temples across the land, let this grass be used in worship, so people will remember that it quenched the deadly fires of Sindura's greed."

And so it is, to this day, that you will find *durva* grass used in the ceremony of worship in all Hindu temples where there is a shrine to Ganesha.

The Wishing Jewel

On the banks of a river, in a small thatched hut among groves of banyan trees, there lived a *rishi*, holy and wise, called Kapila. One day he sat meditating in front of his hut, when a young prince called Kana happened by with a hunting party of a thousand men. Now Kana was the son of a king called Avijita, and he was a young man spoiled by the pleasures of royalty. Shiva himself had once blessed Kana with great fighting strength.

"Welcome to my humble home, young prince," said Kapila. "Will you allow me to honor you and your followers with a feast?"

"A feast?" scoffed Kana, casting a scornful eye upon the thatched roof of Kapila's hut, its threshold bare except for a simple rice flour design drawn upon it by the *rishi*'s wife. "What feast can you give me, old man, in this hovel you call a home? I am born into a royal family and am used to the ways of the court."

Kapila's gaze grew stern, but his voice was calm. "The eye, my son, does not always see all there is," he said. He took from around his neck a golden chain on which there hung a pendant, a gem the size of a walnut. Its many facets caught the sunlight, turned it into the colors of the rainbow and cast them all around the riverbank and on the water, so that the deer, cropping grass, looked up and were dazzled. Kapila held the gem in his hands, closed his eyes, and prayed.

Cries of astonishment arose from Kana and his men. The delicious aroma of a banquet filled the small clearing in front of the *rishi*'s hut. Banana leaves appeared in rows upon the ground, heaped with generous portions of rice, lentils, fresh fruit, and vegetables. There were small leaf-cups of yogurt and sweets and coconut milk.

Kana and his followers ate their fill. They murmured their appreciation. They thanked Kapila, but all the while Kana's eyes followed the magic pendant. Soon it was time for them all to leave. Still Kana's eyes drank in the silvery darting lights of the gemstone.

As he got on his horse, Kana said to Kapila, "Old man, give me that jewel. I can put it to better use than you."

"Prince," said Kapila, his voice hard and cool as a river rock.

"Take your leave. This jewel, the *Chintamani*, is a gift to me from the god Indra, whom once I helped. It has great powers, for it can bring to reality its owner's every wish. It is not yours for the asking."

Kana's men bowed to Kapila, and turned their horses around to leave. But Kana reached down and jerked the pendant off Kapila's neck, whipped his horse away in a cloud of dust, and was gone.

Kapila's eyes were sad as he prayed to Vishnu. "Lord of peace, lord of justice, this is a vain prince indeed," said Kapila, when Vishnu appeared before him. "Tell me what I must do to get the *Chintamani* back from him. With its power and his arrogance, he can do great harm."

Vishnu said to Kapila, "Beware of Prince Kana. He has great strength in battle. It is a gift to him from Shiva. Only Ganesha can help you because only he has powers equal to Shiva's."

So Kapila sat on a great hard rock and meditated upon Ganesha. Soon Ganesha spoke to him in his deepest thoughts.

"I will help you, holy sage," said Ganesha. "The *Chintamani* is a dangerous toy in the hands of a greedy young prince."

As the prince Kana slept one night soon thereafter, he had a strange dream. He was on a battlefield, leading his army of a thousand warriors against the *rishi* Kapila. In the dream, Kapila too had a huge army. Kana's men were beaten back, wave upon wave of them. Then a warrior with an elephant head, surrounded by golden flames and with the strength of a hundred, appeared in Kana's dream. Fear wrapped its chilly arms around Kana's heart, and he awoke trembling.

"I must lead my army against Kapila," said Kana to his father Avijita, "for I fear he will strike first, and then I am doomed."

The old king shook his head in sorrow. "Son of my body," he said to Kana. "I will pray for your victory, but I tremble for you, for I, too, see doom, and it lives in your eyes." Kana brushed aside his father's words, gathered his massive army, and prepared for war. In the morning he led his forces to battle. Just as in the dream, Kapila was waiting for him.

"Prince Kana," said Kapila. "I do not wish to fight with you, but if you want battle, I am ready." He turned to the ranks of warriors lining the riverbank behind him and said, "Noble soldiers sent by Ganesha, may your victory be swift."

The battle was fierce. As Kana's dream had predicted, the warriors who fought for the *rishi* Kapila defeated wave upon wave of Kana's own men. Finally, Kana's generals came to him and said, "Prince, you have no choice. We cannot win against this divine army. Take our advice. Surrender."

Kana set his jaw and threw his head back and laughed a hoarse and desperate laugh. "I would rather die," said he, jumping down from his chariot, gripping his golden bow, and advancing toward Kapila.

Suddenly there was a clap of thunder, and a giant fireball

51

whirled out of the heavens. It swirled and licked its way down. It stopped in front of Kana, scorching his robes and sending beads of sweat down his cheeks. In the midst of the flames was Ganesha.

Kana shot a stream of arrows at Ganesha, but Ganesha swept his noose through the air and the arrows fell to the ground in a heap.

Kana roared with rage, "You pot-bellied creature! How dare you oppose me?" He reached for the *Chintamani*, which hung on its golden chain around his neck. He held it in both hands and shouted, "O jewel of my dreams and wishes, grant me—"

Ganesha's axe flew through the air and felled Kana to the ground, so that his spirit left his body before his wish ever left his lips. A great wail of grief tore through the air as the noble King Avijita ran to his son and knelt by his body weeping, "You grew into a man filled with vanity and greed, but Kana, O Kana, once you were my child."

Ganesha laid a hand upon the old king's head, bowed so low and heavy with sorrow. "Let the world fall silent for a moment," said Ganesha, "so that we may all remember how great a warrior lived as Kana before he was ruined by greed and selfishness. Now his spirit is set free and will not need to be born again."

At once the birds stopped twittering and the crickets stopped chirping and all of creation was quiet for an instant.

King Avijita took the jewel, the *Chintamani*, off the body of his son and handed it to Kapila, saying, "Keep it safe, holy one. It must cause no more war."

Kapila in turn gave the gleaming jewel to Ganesha. "My heart is sick of bloodshed," said he. "Others like Kana may come with evil in their hearts, seeking this bauble. Will you guard it for the world, Ganesha?"

Ganesha laughed, the first sound of cheer on this day of sadness. "I have plenty to hold in my hands," he said, "but I know someone who is loyal and watchful, and who knows just where to hide treasures such as this." And Ganesha handed the *Chintamani* to his trusted mouse, Mushika.

The little mouse gripped the shining jewel in his mouth. His eyes gleamed, his whiskers twitched. He looked up at Ganesha as if to say, "Is our job done for the day, master?" Images of Ganesha and Mushika sometimes show the wishing jewel, the *Chintamani*, in Mushika's mouth, ready to be hidden away from the Kanas of the world.

How Ganga Came to Earth

Parvati, Ganesha's mother, was the daughter of Himavan, king of the mighty Himalaya Mountains. Her sister was Ganga, goddess of the mighty river Ganga. Delighted by Ganga's beauty and wit, the *devas* invited her to come and live with them in their world. There she amused the gods with her spirited ways.

On earth, a king called Sagara, who had ruled with justice and wisdom for many years, decided to hold a grand celebration. As was the custom, he released a white horse to run free and claim for him the land where it might roam. But Indra, king of the *devas*, stole the horse, and as the day wore on, King Sagara's soldiers could find no trace of it.

Now this king had many sons, sixty thousand of them. He sent them to look for the white horse. After much searching, they found it near the hut of the *rishi* called Kapila, who was deep in meditation at the time. In their hurry to get the horse back, Sagara's sons disturbed Kapila. He opened his eyes. So hot was his glance with the power of his meditation that all sixty thousand of the young men were burned to ashes.

Sagara then sent his grandson Amsuman to look for his missing sons. Amsuman found Kapila and the horse. "But what's here?" cried Amsuman. "The royal jewels that my uncles wore! And these, are these their ashes?"

"My son, I did not mean to kill them," said Kapila. "But they disturbed my meditation. I was startled and did not have time to control my powers."

"Holy sage," begged Amsuman, "release their souls."

Kapila said, "Prince, I cannot. Take back your horse; but only the waters of Ganga can wash away these ashes and set your uncles' spirits free."

Amsuman returned to his grandfather, and they prayed to Ganga, pleading with her to come down to earth. Ganga, in the world of the *devas*, would not listen. Sagara and Amsuman, and Amsuman's son, Dilipa, all lived and died without being able to bring Ganga to earth.

When Dilipa's son, Bhagiratha, came to be a man, he vowed, "I will bring Ganga here to free the spirits of my ancestors. This shall be my life's work." He stood on a mountain top in the Himalayas. He meditated for years, until anthills grew over his body and trees planted seeds in his hair. His power grew so great that Brahma and all the *devas* could ignore him no longer.

Brahma finally said to Ganga, "Princess, you must leave here and go to earth, but the earth will be crushed by the force of your waters."

Brahma advised Bhagiratha, "Ask Shiva to receive Ganga on his head, and lower her gently to earth."

Bhagiratha meditated again for a whole year until Shiva agreed to do as he asked.

So the river Ganga began her journey to earth. First she rushed down in a gleeful torrent, crying, "Lord Shiva, beware! I can sweep you away!"

"Impertinent child," muttered Shiva, and trapped her gushing water in his matted hair and refused to let her out.

"Lord of the sacred dance, release her!" begged Bhagiratha. "She meant no harm."

Grumbling, Shiva let Ganga out of his hair, and once again, she began to pour downward. Her swift currents surged with life. Fishes darted about and tadpoles wriggled while river weeds waved in her silvery tides. Birds and insects and tiny water creatures all joyfully descended to earth in Ganga's arms.

Then Ganga made one more mistake. She gushed over the sacred fires of a *rishi*, Jahnu, and put them out. Angry at this interruption of his daily prayer ritual, and furious that the holy

flame had been extinguished, the *rishi* caught Ganga in the palm of his cupped hand. In one mighty sip, he swallowed her rushing waters, fishes and weeds and all, down to the last drop.

Now the *devas* joined with Bhagiratha in pleading with Jahnu for Ganga's freedom. Reluctantly, Jahnu let the waters out through his ear, so that Ganga could at last wash the ashes of Sagara's sons and release their spirits.

While Ganga's waters tumbled at last onto the earth, Ganesha and his brother Muruga held out small clay pots to catch some of the water. As Ganesha held his clay pot, he leaned into Ganga's fresh spray, cold as the tops of the mountains, and took a great deep breath of the clean moist air. Laughing, Ganga splashed and frothed over Ganesha, painting a crescent moon onto his forehead with her cool white foam.

That is how Ganga came to earth. She lives here still, in the form of the river that we know as the Ganga, or Ganges, sweeping in a great arc across the northern plains of India. As for Ganesha, the clay pot is often shown in images and paintings of him. It is held in the curl of his trunk, very carefully, so that Ganga's water does not splash onto the earth without her permission. And her mark of the crescent moon adorns his forehead.

The Crocodile

Ganesha was once born on earth to a *rishi* called Kashyapa and his wife, Aditi, so that he could help them rid the world of a pair of twin *asuras* who were frightening people and destroying forests and animals. Kashyapa and Aditi loved their funny little child with an elephant head, and Ganesha in turn loved them. While he waited to grow up and defeat the *asuras*, he made life joyful for them and for all the people who visited Kashyapa's *ashrama*. His laughter was echoed by the happiness of those who saw him.

One day Aditi was washing clothes by the river, slapping the garments on great flat slabs of rock and pounding them with a wooden board to make them clean and bright. Absorbed in her task, she forgot to keep an eye on the toddler Ganesha. He sat for a while on a rock and dangled his feet in the water, laughing loudly as the water-weeds tickled his heels and the small fishes nibbled at his toes. Then a light breeze, stirring the forest, blew a beautiful heart-shaped leaf off a tree. It danced slowly and gracefully through the air, this way and that, fluttering and dipping with each breath of the breeze. Ganesha clapped his plump little hands and shrieked with delight. The leaf landed gently on the river and floated away, slowly at first, then faster and faster, until it reached the middle of the stream.

"Eeeee!" shouted Ganesha. Before Aditi knew what was happening, he leaped off the rock and splashed his way into the water, reaching out for the leaf. His feet slipped and skidded on the wet rocks of the river bed as he waded in deeper and deeper. The water came up to his middle, then up to his neck.

"Ganesha!" shouted Aditi. "Come back!" Ganesha paid no attention.

Suddenly a rough brown-green body surfaced right next to the fat little child. A broad brown-green tail thrashed the water. A big mouth opened, full of razor teeth. It was a giant crocodile, and it snapped Ganesha up, arms and legs and elephant head and all.

"My child!" screamed Aditi. "Help, help!" A group of women gathering firewood in the forest came running up. They beat sticks together and threw stones at the crocodile.

Meanwhile, Ganesha thrashed and flailed around like a small storm inside the crocodile so that it opened up its huge mouth and spat him out. At once, Ganesha jumped onto the crocodile's back and danced about, leaping happily from tail-tip to nose-tip and back again.

"Come back to shore at once," yelled Aditi. "Come back, my son, my holy child. Ganesha, swim to shore, quickly, quickly!"

"It's Ganesha!" exclaimed the women, and they dropped their firewood and fell to the ground in wonder. Ganesha gurgled with laughter and danced with greater energy on the crocodile's back.

"Look, blessed lady," said one of the women, very soft and slow. "The crocodile is swimming to shore—and he has Ganesha on his back."

Sure enough, the crocodile swam to the bank, flipping the water carefully away from Ganesha, curling its tail up to keep him from falling off. Gently, very gently, it tipped its small burden off its back. Then it bent its head to touch the ground at Ganesha's feet.

Kashyapa had come out to see the commotion. He frowned in anger. "God he may be," said he, "but he is also a child. He needs to learn he cannot go jumping into the river like that and worrying us to death!"

"Sshh," said Aditi. "Just look."

As Kashyapa drew a breath to answer her, there was a flash

like lightning. The crocodile vanished and in his place was a handsome man, smiling and bending to touch Ganesha's feet.

"My name is Chitran," said the man. "In my previous life, I angered the great sage Bhrigu. Busy with the ceremonies at my daughter's wedding, I failed to welcome him and offer him food. He cursed me to be born again as a crocodile. When I fell at his feet and asked for his mercy, he was sorry for me. He told me that only Ganesha's touch could help me shed my crocodile form. So now, my lord Ganesha, you have released me, and I am your servant for all time."

The child Ganesha only laughed and stretched out his arms to Chitran, who lifted him up onto his shoulders and walked back to Kashyapa's *ashrama* with him. Aditi and Kashyapa were left on the riverbank, staring in amazement at their funny, magical child.

Why Ganesha Never Married

When Ganesha grew to be a young man, his parents Parvati and Shiva looked about for a suitable bride for him. In those days men were allowed to marry more than one wife at a time, so Shiva and Parvati settled on two young women named Valli and Devayani, who were both beautiful and spirited.

"How wonderful for us," said Parvati to Shiva. "They will make lovely brides and dear wives to our son."

Shiva and Parvati invited Brahma to be the priest at the ceremony. They consulted the astrologers, who studied the star charts and decided upon a day of good fortune for the wedding.

A thousand artisans and craftsmen worked to

decorate Mount Kailasa for the occasion. A great canopy of flowers was made, and the scent of the *tulasi* plant hung in the cool, crisp air. On the day that Ganesha was to marry, musicians played sweet melodies. The drummers flexed their fingers as they got ready to play loud and hard, loud and hard, to drown out any evil words or sounds at the sacred ceremony.

In the midst of all this joy, one person was unhappy. Ganga sat sulking in a corner. "Why, sister, such a sour look," said Parvati, "on such a happy day?"

But Ganga frowned and said, "My Bhishma, my son, is a bachelor and will be one for all his life. It grieves me that your Ganesha with his elephant head and his fat belly will marry such beautiful young women." She looked up to see if Parvati had heard, but Parvati had gone to make sure the cooks had enough cardamom for the wedding sweets, and had not waited for her reply.

Annoyed, Ganga tossed her long tresses and swept off down the mountainside. "I'll see about this wedding," said she, casting a rock or two down the slopes on her way.

It was time for all the family to have ceremonial baths. They rubbed their bodies down with sesame oil until they glowed with its heat. Then Shiva called to his great bull Nandi, "Fetch us cool water from the well, Nandi, so we may get ready. The hour draws near for Ganesha's marriage."

Nandi looked in the well. "Master," he called back, "the well is empty. I'll get water from the stream instead."

Nandi plodded to the stream that usually chattered and gurgled its way over polished rocks and waving ferns. "Master!" he called, and his voice was worried. "The stream is dry."

Nandi ran down the mountain to the river in the valley below. Just as he reached it, the last drops of water from the river drained away, down, down, toward the great plains, until they were lost in the salty wastes of the ocean. In the distance was Ganga, racing swiftly away, taking with her all the water from wells and streams, rivers and waterfalls.

Finally, Nandi reached the ocean. "Where will you go now, goddess?" he asked, as he waded into the water. "This water is salty, but water it is, and I will take it back to Kailasa for Ganesha's wedding."

"There will be no wedding," shouted Ganga, and she caught hold of Nandi's ankles and held him as fast as the earth holds the roots of a tree. Try as he might, he could not get loose.

On Mount Kailasa, Brahma shook his head. "There will be no wedding," he said to Shiva. "There can be no wedding until we have all bathed. Something tells me this is Ganga's doing."

Shiva's brow grew dark, and he paced up and down, frowning. But the great sage Brihaspati, for whom a day and a planet are named, said, "The hour is past. Each of our futures is written in our souls, and marriage is not in Ganesha's future."

"It's all Ganga's fault," said Shiva sternly.

Brihaspati said, "Ganga is merely the one who made this true. Had she not drained the water and made it impossible for

you to bathe, something else would have happened to prevent this wedding."

"What of Valli and Devayani?" asked Parvati. "And what about Ganesha? Will he be happy, never to wed?"

"My mother," said Ganesha. "If it is not in my stars to be a husband, I will find joy in being a *brahmachari*, a bachelor. I will find another way to serve the world. If Valli and Devayani do not object, perhaps they can marry my brother Muruga."

So Ganesha never married, and Muruga got two wives where before he had none, and Ganga returned the rushing, tumbling, silvery waters to the slopes of Kailasa. At least, that is how some people tell the story.

The Old Young Woman and Her Songs

To very poor parents who had no food to eat there once was born a little baby girl. Weeping, they wrapped her in rags and left her under a banyan tree, saying, "May someone with a kind heart find you and give you a better life than we can."

A family of wandering minstrels heard the infant's cries and marvelled at the sound. "Hark," said the man among them. "That baby has a voice like temple bells."

"Who could have abandoned such a one?" wondered the woman. "Let's take her with us and make her ours, so she can sing and give us joy."

The children in the family said, "Yes, yes, let's take her with us, she'll be our little sister."

The Old Young Woman and Her Songs

So the family of minstrels picked up the baby girl and took her with them on their travels. They loved her and raised her as their own. As she grew in age and strength, her voice became more and more beautiful, and all the world could tell that there was music in her soul. She loved to walk along riverbanks, gathering flowers of different colors: white jasmine buds, barely opened, with perfume that could stir the hardest heart; and pink frangipani blossoms with centers of deep, swirling red. She would take her handful of flowers to the Ganesha shrine at a nearby temple. There she would spend hours in prayer, offering to Ganesha her flowers and the songs she sang in her clear, beautiful voice that was like a temple bell.

Soon, very soon, the girl grew into a woman, and she was as lovely as her voice. "Come here, my princess," her adoptive mother would say to her. "Let me comb your hair." And she would untangle and braid the long black hair until it shone like a raven's feathers.

The young woman was careless about her appearance, and her mother would sometimes scold her, saying, "Don't wander about in the sun, child," or "You forgot to grind turmeric paste and rub it on your cheeks. Your skin will be dry like an old woman's and then who will marry you?" But the girl-now-a-woman had another dream to dream, and she spent all her free time collecting flowers for Ganesha and singing to him in her voice like a temple bell.

One day the mother said, "My daughter, let us find you a

husband, a young man who is hard-working and warm-hearted, from a good family, whose birth star is one of good fortune, so you may have a happy home to live in as a woman."

"*Amma*," replied the young woman, and her dream was in her eyes, and her thoughts were far away. "I don't want to marry. I want to sing the songs in my heart, the songs of Ganesha. I will wander the land and sing my songs for as long as I live."

The mother was horrified. "Thoughtless child!" she cried. "We have raised you and cared for you, and now you want to throw it all away? What kind of life will you have, wandering about on your own? You will starve to death. Is this why we rescued you from under that banyan tree so many years ago?" The mother began to weep. But the young woman raised her voice in song. She sang about Ganesha, of his wisdom and his knowledge of the forces of life and death, and of the clean, clear path he cuts with his axe, the path that leads to truth. In spite of herself, the mother, listening, was comforted.

Within days, however, the mother's comfort turned again to worry, and she said to her husband, "We must find a good match for our beautiful child of the banyan tree. If we could only find the right young man, I am sure this Ganesha madness of hers would pass. Talk to the elders of each village through which we travel."

As time went by and the parents searched for a bridegroom, word of the young woman's beauty and grace began to spread, and the line of suitors for her hand grew and grew. In every village her family visited, and stayed, and sang, she turned dozens of young men away.

"Oh, take this one!" cried the mother in despair. "He's rich. Perhaps he'll let you sing if that's what you want to do, foolish one." Or, "That one, now! He is born under the star called Avittam. People born under that star can turn cauldrons of lead into gold. Say yes, child, say yes."

"No, *Amma*," said the young woman. "I told you. I'll marry no one."

Finally, one day, the young woman could stand it no more. She raced to the Ganesha shrine and threw herself down at the feet of the great stone image, crying, "Enough! Take my youth away from me! Take my beauty, it's a curse. When people see it they can't see beyond it, they can't see what is within me. Oh, give me wrinkles and give me old age, Ganesha, so I can live the life I want to live." And the young woman wept most bitterly, and her tears washed the feet of the great stone Ganesha.

Suddenly a resounding chuckle broke into the sound of her sobbing, and a voice as deep and cool and dark as the heart of a granite carving said to her, "Are you sure, *Auvaiyar*, respected old one?"

Startled, the woman sat up, and raised a trembling hand to her face. The smooth young skin had given way to soft, gentle wrinkles. She pulled over her shoulder the long braid of hair that usually hung down her back to her waist. It was a gleaming silvery white. She looked at her hand, and it had the leathery strength that comes from decades of work.

"Thank you, Lord Ganesha, with all my heart," she cried.

"You're certain this is what you want?" said Ganesha sternly. "If you want to change your mind, you'd best do it now, or else spend a lifetime in regret and sorrow."

The woman raised shining eyes to Ganesha. She opened her mouth and sang her gratitude to him. Her voice was steady and clear, and her words were filled with confidence. For the rest of her years, and they were many, people called her *Auvaiyar*, which means "respected old one." She travelled through the villages and towns of the Tamil-speaking parts of what we know today as southern India, singing songs about Ganesha, teaching the people, and helping them to heal their sorrows through her words of wisdom.

Today, Auvaiyar's songs are still sung in celebration of the woman who had the courage to seek her own path, and the elephant-faced god who helped her follow it.

The River Kaveri

Once there was a terrible drought in the southern part of the land we now call India. The wells ran dry; the crops shrivelled and died. Even mighty tamarind trees drooped until their feathery leaves grew yellow and brushed the dusty ground. People ate their seed-grain, and children cried with hunger.

Saddened by the suffering of the people, the *rishi* Agastya prayed to Brahma. "Go north to Shiva's home," said Brahma, "and fetch from there the sacred waters of the snows that never die. With the water you will begin a new river to quench the thirst of this hot land."

So Agastya travelled north until his feet were sore with walking and his eyes were red with the dust of the road. Finally, he reached Kailasa, filled his pot with the sacred water, and returned the way he had come. He climbed the hills of the place that is now called Coorg and stopped to catch his breath.

"I must find a good place to make the river start," thought Agastya when he was rested. He looked for a safe spot to set down the precious pot of water. Playing in the dirt nearby was a little boy, dusty-faced and dressed in rags.

"Here, small one," called Agastya. "Hold this pot for me."

"Why?" asked the boy, his eyes wide at Agastya's tangled white hair and his uncombed beard.

"Never mind, you little rascal, just do as you're told," said Agastya. "Hold it in both hands and don't spill a drop!"

Agastya looked about him and began measuring the land with a careful gaze.

"Perhaps over there," he said out loud. "No, too flat. Here? Too many rocks. Hmmm . . ." Agastya paced up and down, thinking deeply.

Meanwhile the boy, who was really Ganesha in disguise, picked a place, put the pot down, and went away.

After some time, unable to make up his mind, Agastya called out, "I cannot decide. What do you think, my small helper?"

There was silence. Agastya looked around. "Where are you, child?" he cried. "Why did you put the pot down?"

All at once, a big crow came swishing out of the sky on shiny black wings. It perched roughly on the edge of the pot, clattering its pointed claws against the clay. The pot rocked, tipped, and spilled its precious water onto the ground.

Agastya was livid. He shook his fist at the crow. "Evil creature," he cried. "Shiva's curse will be upon you for upsetting my pot."

A bright light shone for an instant, making Agastya blink. The crow disappeared. In its place, rosy-faced, trunk waving in greeting, was Ganesha.

"A curse, you say?" said Ganesha with a chuckle. "Upon me? Why, all I did was start your river for you."

"Ganesha with ears like fly whisks, was it really you? And the child? Was that you too?" Agastya's anger blossomed into smiles.

Ganesha nodded. His large ears nodded with him. His laughter echoed through the southern lands, as the river Kaveri gurgled out of Agastya's pot. Her trickle as she touched the ground grew into a stream, and then into a torrent, as she rushed down the hills of Coorg, bringing life again to the thirsty fields and villages below. You can still find her there, running down the hillside and snaking her way across the peninsula, until she leaps into the warm, deep waters of the Bay of Bengal.

As for the people of the land, they still tell of how Agastya brought Kaveri all the way south from the Himalaya Mountains, but then became so tired and preoccupied that he could not recognize Ganesha when he saw him. So remember, they say, that when you think Ganesha is hindering you in your work, perhaps he is really helping.

The
Birth
of Phagpa

In Tibet in the thirteenth century an anxious husband awaited the birth of a baby. As his wife grew restless and felt the time of birth drawing near, the husband could not be still. He paced up and down like a caged snow leopard, until finally the midwife who had arrived to help with the birth said to him, "Your woman has work to do, and so do I. Be off with you!"

The man's wife said to him, "My husband, go light a butter lamp at the temple. Then meditate and rest your spirit."

"I will," said the weary man, "but O my wife, there is no butter."

"You will have to milk the *dri* and make the

butter," she said to him. "Though that is woman's work, still you must do it, because I cannot."

The man took a wooden bucket outside their mountain hut, and milked the patient *dri* that stood tethered there, and the milk was rich with butterfat. He lit a fire and boiled it and scooped off the creamy skin that gathered on its surface. He spilled a lot and saved a little. "I am clumsy, wife," said he. "This is harder work than I imagined."

The man's wife did not reply. She breathed deeply and smiled and waited.

Then the man took a wooden paddle and churned butter from the cream. All this work calmed his racing heart, and as his wife settled into the work of childbirth, he took the butter and went to the temple and lit a lamp. The shrine of Buddha and of gods old and new was quiet in the purple sunset. The man sat down in the lotus position and meditated upon Ganesha.

"*Log den*, lord of obstacles, may the birth of my child be safe," he prayed.

Like a thought that floats into the mind, Ganesha came to the young husband and smiled at him.

"Look down," said Ganesha.

For a moment the man forgot to breathe, so startled was he to find that Ganesha had taken him high, high up on the crest of Mount Meru, the sacred mountain where the herbs of healing grow and the springs hold the waters of purity. Like a cloth winding off a loom, a magic land lay spread out beneath.

"What is that land?" asked the man. "I have never seen such a country before."

Ganesha showed him the land of Mongolia, saying to him, "The son your wife will bear will conquer this land."

"He will be a great hero, then?" asked the man humbly, for he had not much courage and could hardly believe that a son of his would be a mighty warrior.

"A hero, no," laughed Ganesha. "He will be a man of peace. He will conquer the hearts and minds of the people in that land, even the emperor himself, the great Kublai. He will take to them all the teachings of Buddha."

The man's heart pounded again, this time with joy. He joined his hands in gratitude and respect and bowed low, saying, "You have eased my fears, Ganesha. I have joyful news to take to my wife."

There was no answer and when the man looked up, he was alone. The rough touch of a mud-plastered wall on his back told him that he was home again. He cut a thorny branch from a rose bush that flowered pink and wild and laid it across his doorstep to keep evil spirits away. On top of the branch he arranged a *towo*, three stones for good luck, one on top of the other. Then he stepped carefully over the threshold.

"Oh, look, my beautiful little mother," cried the midwife. "You have a baby boy!" A loud and breathless wail told the man that a soul had once again been born on earth, and he rushed inside the hut with his arms outstretched to hold his son.

The Birth of Phagpa

The son born that day to the man and his wife grew up to be the Tibetan saint Phagpa. And just as Ganesha predicted, he took the teachings of Buddhism to the people of Mongolia, far away across the purple mountains.

In the Beginning

When the Great Spirit that is the spirit of everything caused creation to happen, the world was formless and was only energy. Then Brahma, Vishnu, and Shiva were created, but still there were no worlds to live in, no *devas*, no *asuras*, no people. There was darkness, no light; silence, no sound.

Then slowly, sound began, and it was the sound of *Om*. At first it was very soft, a faint whisper. Then it began growing louder and louder until it echoed through the nothingness. As its volume grew great it brought with it the first pale light of the first pale dawn, and as the sound grew, the dawn grew too, into colors that were new and quickly changing.

Then out of the dawn came Ganesha. In his dancing form he came, blowing his conch, blowing the sound of *Om* into all the corners of the new dawn. He whirled and swirled, and from the light and sound came movement.

"Come!" cried Ganesha to the Three, to Brahma, Vishnu, and Shiva. "Come, there are worlds to be created, to be saved, to be destroyed."

But the Three did not know how to begin.

"I will show you," said Ganesha. "I am the universe itself, and I will show you." And he opened his mouth into a cave, gigantic and warm, and swallowed Brahma, Vishnu, and Shiva.

Inside Ganesha's belly they saw worlds reflected, and they saw time stretching forward and back and upon itself. They saw space. They saw suns burning brightly, and planets whirling in their orbits, as Ganesha had whirled when first he came dancing out of the dawn.

"Now I know what I should create," said Brahma, "but still I do not know how to begin."

Ganesha's belly thundered with his laughter, and the universes within him heaved to and fro in the chaos that would become creation.

"You have forgotten to meditate," he told Brahma, Vishnu, and Shiva. "And you must speak the word *Om*, for it is the beginning and the end, and everything in between."

Then the Three meditated on Ganesha and chanted the sacred sound of *Om*, and soon Ganesha opened his mouth and

released them. For a while they were in a trance, filled with the echoes of *Om*. Presently, for time had now begun, they were able to start their tasks of creating, preserving, and destroying universes, time after time after time. They are at it still.

Pronunciation Guide

Most of the character names and italicized words in these stories come from Sanskrit. Occasionally one is from another Indian language, such as Tamil. The following are some general rules for Sanskrit pronunciation:

The letter *a* in Sanskrit is sometimes pronounced long, as in *father*. Sometimes it is pronounced like a short *u*, as in *but*. (See *A*disesh*a*, where the first *a* is long, the second short.)

The letter *e* is pronounced like an English *ay*, as in *bay*. (See Adis*e*sha.)

The letter *i* is pronounced like *ee*, as in *meet*. (See D*i*lipa.)

The letter *o* is close to an English *o* as in *ghost*. (See Deval*o*ka.)

The letter *u* is pronounced *oo* as in *foot* (e.g., *U*ma.)

The letters *ri* are considered one letter in Sanskrit, and that letter is a vowel. Pronounce it like the *ri* in *river*, but with a very short *i* sound. (See *Ri*shi.)

The letter *d* is sometimes a hard *d*, as in *day*, sometimes a soft *th* as in *this*. (See Nan*d*i.)

Some consonants with an *h* after them are pronounced in a special way: *kh* as in *dark-haired* (see Gajamu*kh*asura); *bh* as in *abhor* (see A*bh*aya mudra).

Finally, in Sanskrit, as in many Indian languages, all syllables of a word receive equal emphasis.

Ganesha's Names

Ganesha has more than 100 names. Here are just a few of them:

Ekadanta (Ay-kuh-dun-thuh): One-tusk

Gajakarnika (Guh-juh-kur-nee-kuh): Elephant Ears

Gajamukha (Guh-juh-moo-khuh): Elephant Face

Gajanana (Guh-jah-nuh-nuh): Elephant Headed

Ganapati (Guh-nuh-puh-thee): Leader of the Ganas (guh-nuh), Shiva's followers

Ganesha (Guh-nay-shuh): Lord of the Ganas

Lambodara (Lum-boh-thuh-ruh): Big Bellied

Sumukha (Soo-moo-khuh): Beautiful Face

Vakratunda (Vuh-kruh-thoon-duh): Curved Tusk

Vighnaraja (Veeg-nuh-rah-juh): King of Obstacles

Vinayaka (Vee-nah-yuh-kuh): Supreme Leader, or one who has no leader

Gods and People, Kings and Demons: A List of Characters

Adisesha (Ahdi-say-shuh): The serpent on whose coils Vishnu sleeps.

Agastya (Uh-gusth-yuh): The *rishi* who helped bring the river Kaveri to earth.

Airavata (Eye-rah-vuh-thuh): Indra's six-tusked elephant.

Amsuman (Um-soo-mahn): Grandfather of Bhagiratha, the king who brought Ganga down to earth.

Auvaiyar (Uhv-vuy-yahr): A ninth-century Tamil saint.

Avijita (Uh-vee-jee-thuh): A king whose son was killed in battle by Ganesha.

Bhagiratha (Bhah-gee-ruh-thuh): The king whose prayers and meditation brought the holy river Ganga down to earth.

Brahma (Bruh-muh): Creator of the universe.

Chandra (Chun-thruh): God of the moon. He rides in a two- or three-wheeled chariot across the night skies, holding white lotuses in his two hands. His images generally show a face and two hands but no body.

Dilipa (Dee-lee-puh): Father of Bhagiratha, who brought Ganga to earth.

Gajamukhasura (Guh-juh-moo-khah-soo-ruh): Demon with the face of an elephant who fought with Ganesha and was defeated by him.

Ganga (Gun-gah): Parvati's sister, goddess of the river Ganga or Ganges.

Himavan (Hee-muh-vahn): King of the mountains we know as the Himalaya.

Indra (In-thruh): King of the *devas*, or gods.

Kana (Kah-nuh): The greedy prince who was killed in battle with Ganesha.

Kapila (Kuh-pi-luh): A *rishi* with extraordinary powers gained through prayer and meditation.

Kaveri (Kah-vay-ree): River in southern India, one of the seven sacred rivers in the Hindu tradition.

Kubera (Koo-bear-uh): God of wealth, rich beyond imagination, king of the Yakshas (Yuk-shuhs), a race of spirits or demi-gods. Kubera is sometimes depicted riding on a man's shoulders or in a cart drawn by men, to show how people are burdened by their attachment to wealth.

Muruga (Moo-roo-guh): Ganesha's brother, also called Kumara (Koo-mah-ruh) or Skanda (Skun-thuh). He rides a peacock and is sometimes shown with six heads, representing the five senses and the mind that tries to control them.

Mushika: (Moo-shi-kuh): A mouse, Ganesha's mount.

Nandi (Nun-thee): Shiva's mount, a great white bull.

Parvati (Pahr-vuh-thee): Her other name is Uma, "the bright one." The *Puranas*, ancient Hindu texts, describe her as Vishnu's sister. She is Ganesha's mother and Shiva's wife and the daughter of Himavan, king of the Himalaya Mountains. Her younger sister is the river goddess Ganga. Parvati has many forms, some calm and nurturing, some angry and vengeful.

Phagpa (Phahg-pah): The thirteenth-century Tibetan scholar and ambassador who converted the famous Mongol emperor Kublai Khan to Buddhism.

Saraswati (Suh-ruh-svuh-thee): Goddess of knowledge, Brahma's wife. On her special day each year, Hindu children must put aside books, pens, pencils, paper, musical instruments and all things that have to do with knowledge and the arts so that Saraswati may bless these things. Saraswati sits on a lotus, holding a *veena* (an Indian lute), sacred beads, and a book.

Shiva (Shi-vuh): God of destruction, Ganesha's father.

Sindura (Sin-thoo-ruh): The demon to whom Brahma makes an ill-judged promise in "In His Belly." This story has several versions. In one, Sindura threatens Shiva and Parvati and is destroyed by Ganesha's axe.

Vishnu (Vish-noo): God who preserves or sustains the universe.

Vyasa (Viyah-suh): Learned poet who composed the Hindu epic called the *Mahabharata*. He is also the composer of other sacred Hindu texts, and is said to have divided the *Vedas* into the four parts that are studied today by religious and scholarly Hindus. Each age is supposed to have a Vyasa, a chronicler of the time.

Glossary

Abhaya mudra (Uh-bhu-yuh mood-ruh): A position of the hands in the classical Indian dance form known as Bharatanatyam; indicates protection or blessing. *Abhaya* in Sanskrit means "without fear."

Amma (Um-mah): Mother (in Tamil, the language spoken in the southern part of India).

Ashrama (Ah-shruh-muh): A hermitage, home of a rishi.

Asura (Uh-soo-ruh): A demon.

Asuraloka (Uh-soo-ruh-lo-kuh): World or home of the asuras.

Bharatanatyam (Bhu-ruh-thuh-naht-yum): Classical dance, originating in the southern part of India.

Deva (Day-vuh): A god.

Devaloka (Day-vuh-lo-kuh): World or home of the gods.

Dri (Dree): Female yak, an ox-like mammal. Tibetans drink the
   dri's milk and use it in cooking (Tibetan).

Durva (Door-vuh): Sacred grass used in Ganesha's worship.

Ganapathya (Guh-nuh-puth-yuh): A religious sect of Hindus
   who worship Ganesha as the supreme god.

Ganesha Chaturthi (Guh-nay-shuh Chuh-thoor-thee): Holiday
   special to Ganesha, the fourth night after the new moon in
   August or September. *Chatur* (chuh-thoor) in Sanskrit
   means "four."

Ganeshini (Guh-nay-shi-nee): Female form of Ganesha, repre-
   sented in sculpture but not in mythology.

Karma (Kuhr-muh): Deed or action; the belief that actions have
   consequences across many lifetimes.

Log den (Lohg-den): Lord of obstacles, Tibetan name for
   Ganesha (Tibetan).

Modaka (Moh-duh-kuh): Sweet dumpling special to Ganesha.

Namaste (Nuh-mus-thay): Gesture of greeting, with palms together as in prayer. It is a common mode of greeting in
   India, and means "I bow to the divine in you."

Rishi (Ri-shee): Holy man or saint who has renounced the
   world.

Pal payasam (Pahl pah-yuh-sum): Rice pudding with saffron,
   cardamom and nuts (Tamil).

Rudraksha (Rood-rah-kshuh): Seed from a tree, used in strings
   of prayer beads.

Sanskrit (Sun-skrit): Ancient Indo-European language, used

even today in Hindu worship. Like Latin, Sanskrit is no longer a commonly spoken language, though many Indian languages are descended from it.

Swastika (Swus-thi-kuh): Ancient Hindu symbol of eternal life.

Tulasi (Thoo-luh-see): The holy basil plant, used in Hindu ceremonies and in worship as well as in traditional medicine.

Towo (Thoh-woh): In parts of Tibet, an arrangement of three stones, one on top of the other, to ward off bad luck (Tibetan).

Veda (Vay-thuh): Sacred Hindu text. There are four Vedas, and orthodox Hindus follow the traditions laid down in one or the other of them.

Yoga (Yo-guh): Study of different branches of knowledge. *Hatha yoga* (Huh-thuh yo-guh) is the branch concerned with physical exercise and health. Other branches of yoga relate to, for example, work and prayer.

Sources

Buck, William, reteller. *Mahabharata*. Berkeley: University of California Press, 1973.

Brown, Robert L., ed. *Ganesh: Studies of an Asian God*. Albany: SUNY Press, 1991.

Coomaraswamy, Ananda K., and Sister Nivedita. *Myths of the Hindus and Buddhists*. New York: Dover Publications, 1967.

Courtright, Paul B. *Ganesa: Lord of Obstacles, Lord of Beginnings*. New York: Oxford University Press, 1985.

Getty, Alice. *Ganesa: A Monograph on the Elephant-Faced God*. 2d ed. New Delhi: Munshiram Manoharlal, 1971. ("The Birth of Phagpa" is adapted from this book by permission of the publisher).

Swami Harshananda. *Hindu gods & goddesses*. Madras: Sri Ramakrishna Math, 1982.

Jagannathan, Shakunthala, and Nanditha Krishna. *Ganesha, the Auspicious, the Beginning.* Bombay: Vakils, Feffer & Simons, 1992. ("The Cat" and "In the Beginning" are adapted from this book by permission of the authors).

Jest, Corneille. *Tales of the Turquoise: A Pilgrimage in Dolpo.* Translated from the French by Margaret Stein. Kathmandu, Nepal: Mandala Book Point, 1993.

Nath, Amarendra. *Buddhist Images and Narratives.* New Delhi: Books & Books, 1986.

O'Flaherty, Wendy Doniger. *Hindu Myths: A Sourcebook.* Translated from the Sanskrit. Baltimore: Penguin, 1975.

Ramachandra Rao, S. G. *Ganesa-Kosha.* Bangalore, India: Kalpatharu Research Academy, 1992.

Rajagopalachari, C., reteller. *Mahabharata.* 26th ed. Bombay: Bharatiya Vidya Bhavan, 1985.

Subramuniyaswami, Sivaya. *Lord Ganesha: Benevolent Deity for the Modern Hindu World.* Concord, CA: Himalayan Academy, 1989. ("The Old Young Woman & Her Songs" is adapted from this book by permission of the publisher).

Acknowledgments

I am grateful to the many people who helped make this book possible: To Sri D. L. Narayanachar of Sri Siva Vishnu Temple, Lanham, Maryland, who gave freely and patiently of his time and wisdom; and to Acharya Palaniswami of *Hinduism Today* for addressing my many questions and concerns, and for his gentle and unerring critique of my manuscript; to Arun and Sudha Mehta of Vakils, Bombay, for their kindness and generosity; to Dr. Thunga Satyapal and Dr. Chandrika Prasad, for assistance with the pronunciation guide and Devanagari text. Thanks also to my sternest and most loyal critics, my husband Sumant and my son Nikhil; to Gayatri Mani for pointing me toward some stories I'd forgotten I knew; to my mother-in-law, Hema Krishnaswamy, for her insights that helped me find the "feel" of these myths; to Sally Davies and my writer's group; to Phoebe Bacon for the librarian's perspective; to Terry Sayler, for her help in locating books and source materials; and especially to Diantha Thorpe of Linnet Books for sharing my belief that Ganesha would dance within these pages.

Source materials for this work were obtained courtesy of the University of Maryland's McKeldin Library; the Himalayan Academy/*Hinduism Today*; and the Smithsonian Institution's Arthur M. Sackler Gallery. Permissions to adapt the stories "The Cat," "In the Beginning," "The Old Young Woman and Her Songs," and "The Birth of Phagpa" are as cited with the sources. Where no specific source is cited, the story has been retold from an oral rendering.

Two graphic designs, Ganesha in Lotus and Sanskrit "Om," have been used courtesy of the Himalayan Academy/*Hinduism Today*.